THIS

BOOK

BELONGS

TO *JESSE-LEE*

DISNEY's
SMALL WORLD LIBRARY
PAINTING THE TOWN
An Adventure in France

GROLIER ENTERPRISES INC.
DANBURY, CONNECTICUT

Printed in the United States of America.
Developed by The Walt Disney Company in conjunction with Nancy Hall, Inc.
ISBN 0-7172-8208-2

When Mickey and Goofy decided they wanted to learn to paint, they flew straight to the center of great art—Paris, France.

As they stepped off the plane Mickey sighed. "I can hardly believe we're in Paris! Soon we'll be seeing the sights that inspired great painters like Degas, Renoir, and Matisse!"

"Gawrsh, Mickey, do you think we'll ever be as good as they were?" Goofy asked.

"We can try," Mickey answered with a smile.

The next morning, Mickey and Goofy visited the famous Louvre Museum.

"I've never seen so many great paintings in the same place," Mickey whispered. "Look, there's a Degas painting of ballerinas." Mickey read from the guidebook,

"Degas used to go backstage at the ballet to paint the performers behind the scenes." He paused. "Goofy, are you listening?"

Goofy wasn't listening. He was lost in a dream. He imagined himself as The Great Goofy, whose paintings were exhibited and admired at the Louvre.

"Come on, Mickey," Goofy said with excitement. "Let's get started."

Mickey agreed happily.

After they left the museum, Goofy stopped at a clothing store.

"What are you doing?" Mickey asked.

"You'll see," said Goofy.

When Goofy came out, he was wearing a new smock, beret, and tie.

"Wow, Goofy!" Mickey said. "At least you look like a great artist."

"That's the idea, Mick," said Goofy. "Come on—let's go to the ballet. I want to paint a ballerina, just like Degas did."

Mickey and Goofy arrived in time for the ballet's dress rehearsal. Goofy set up his easel backstage. He could hear the sounds of the orchestra tuning up. It was almost time for the ballet to begin. Excited dancers added the finishing touches to their makeup and adjusted their satin toe shoes.

Goofy couldn't wait to start painting, but the cap of the paint tube wouldn't budge. Goofy struggled mightily. Finally the cap popped off, and paint squirted all over a ballerina.

Goofy felt terrible, but the rehearsal went on. Goofy tried to wipe the paint off the dancer, but the more he wiped, the more it spread. And it was hard to keep up with her as she leaped about the stage.

"Gawrsh, being an artist isn't as easy as it looks," Goofy said later, sighing.

"I think I know what the problem is," Mickey said. "We shouldn't try to paint like Degas. We have to figure out what is the best thing for us to paint. I don't think ballet is the right subject for us, Goofy. Let's find our way back to the hotel and think about it."

The next day, Mickey and Goofy set out to see the Eiffel Tower. There, they met a young Parisian boy named Jacques who was admiring the tower, too. Mickey and Goofy introduced themselves and told Jacques how they had come to Paris to be painters.

"I want to be an architect," Jacques said. "Someday, when I grow up, I will design a building as magnificent as this. And just as they named the tower after its designer, Alexandre Eiffel, they will name my building after me!" he told them.

Mickey and Goofy looked at each other, and they said, "Let's paint the Eiffel Tower!"

"What a wonderful idea! May I watch?" Jacques asked.

"Sure!" they told him as they set up their easels and paints.

Mickey and Goofy painted and painted. Before long the two painters declared they were finished.

"But, *mes amis* . . ." Jacques began.

As soon as Mickey and Goofy held up their paintings, the problem became clear to them, too.

Neither Mickey nor Goofy had been able to fit the entire tower onto one canvas!

"What will we paint now?" Goofy asked.

Jacques suggested painting the flowers at the Luxembourg Gardens, and told Mickey and Goofy how to get there.

"It was nice to meet you," Mickey said. "Would you like to get together in a few days to see our paintings?" The new friends arranged to meet later that week at the Café Rouge.

At the Luxembourg Gardens, Mickey and Goofy met
a little girl named Simone. She loved to sit among the
flowers in the park and read and meet new friends.
"These gardens are perfect!" Goofy sighed.
Mickey agreed. The two set up their easels beside
Simone, so they could talk to her while they painted.

Goofy was so busy painting and talking that he didn't see a bee land on his canvas. Unfortunately, the bee noticed when Goofy painted him pink. The angry bee chased Goofy all around the gardens.

"I don't think this is the right place for us to paint, either," said Mickey.

"I hope your paintings turn out well," said Simone.

"Would you like to see for yourself?" asked Mickey. "We're meeting a friend later this week at the Café Rouge. Would you like to join us?"

Simone agreed happily.

As Mickey and Goofy left the gardens, Goofy realized he was very hungry.

"Gawrsh, Mickey, is this what they mean by a starving artist?" he asked.

Mickey laughed and pointed to a restaurant. "We could stop in there for a bite to eat," he replied.

But as Mickey and Goofy approached the restaurant, they noticed the restaurant owner pointing to the sign showing that the restaurant was closed.

The man opened the door. "We're closed now," he told them, "but I see you are artists. Come in."

The man introduced himself as François, the chef and owner of Chez François.

"The art of cooking is not my only talent," he said proudly. "I am just beginning a still-life painting."

Mickey and François were soon deep in a discussion about the best angle from which to paint the carefully arranged plate of food. Goofy, however, was busy studying the food.

Suddenly Mickey looked from the near-empty plate of food to Goofy's bulging cheeks. Mickey apologized to François, who assured him that he could arrange another plate.

"Thanks very much," said Mickey, "but we'd like to make it up to you. Would you care to join us later this week at the Café Rouge?"

"I would be delighted," said François.

Then Mickey and Goofy decided it was time to go to one of the cafés in the Latin Quarter. The café was crowded, so they shared a table with Michel, a young university student who was also very interested in painting.

As Goofy munched a crusty ham-and-cheese sandwich and an éclair, Michel told them, "France's greatest artists, writers, and thinkers have always met to discuss their work at places like this one."

"This café is what Paris is all about!" Mickey declared. "We'll paint here!"

Goofy looked around the crowded café and daydreamed how one day people would say, "This is where The Great Goofy got his start." He was so busy dreaming that he didn't notice what he was doing. Instead of dipping his paintbrush in his paints, he dipped it in someone's soup.

When Mickey realized what had happened, he hastily apologized to the angry customer. Then he hurried Goofy out of the café, but not before inviting Michel to join them and their other new friends later that week.

Mickey and Goofy wandered through Paris until they came to the bank of the river Seine. There, they saw many artists painting the pretty reflections of the sky on the water. Mickey made friends with a young artist named Monique while Goofy struggled to open his easel.

"Isn't this beautiful?" Monique sighed.

Mickey had to agree, it was a lovely sight—and the perfect picture to paint of Paris. Mickey turned to ask Goofy what he thought of the view.

In his struggle to open the easel, Goofy flew backward against the artist behind him, who fell back against the artist behind him! Paint from their palettes turned the river into a rainbow of color.

Monique helped Mickey and Goofy clean up the mess.

"We should probably get back to the hotel now, anyway," Mickey said to Monique, "but we did enjoy meeting you. Would you care to join us later this week at the Café Rouge?"

Monique was pleased to accept. She wrote down the address of the café and bid Mickey and Goofy farewell.

Refusing to be discouraged, the two friends started out the next day, sure that they would find something special to paint. As they wandered along the busy Paris streets they came to the Arc de Triomphe.

"The guidebook says this arch is located in the heart of Paris. It is called the 'arch of the star' because twelve avenues lead out from the center like the rays of a star," Mickey told Goofy.

"The heart of Paris" was all Goofy heard. "Let's paint the arch!" he said. He hurried to set up his easel. Cars everywhere began to honk their horns loudly.

"Goofy, I don't think this is the time or the place to paint," Mickey said, leading Goofy out of the busy street.

"I don't think we're ever going to find that special something to paint," Goofy admitted. "We don't really know Paris the way all the friends we've made do."

"I've got it!" cried Mickey. "I know just what to paint." Then he told Goofy his plan, and the two went off to paint what was special to them about Paris.

On the last day of their stay, Mickey and Goofy excitedly awaited the arrival of their friends. They couldn't wait to show them their painting.

As the last guest arrived at the Café Rouge, Goofy unveiled the painting. The friends applauded when they saw what Mickey and Goofy had painted. It was a portrait of all of them, and it was wonderful.

"What we finally figured out," Mickey explained, "is that it's best to paint something special—and all of you are what has made France so special to us."

Did You Know...?

There are many different customs and places that make each country special. Do you remember some of the things below from the story?

The Concorde is one of the fastest airplanes in the world. It can fly from Paris to New York City in three hours and forty-five minutes. A regular flight takes at least eight hours.

The Eiffel Tower is the most famous structure in Paris. It was designed by Alexandre Gustave Eiffel, who built the framework for the Statue of Liberty that stands in the harbor of New York City.

Mickey and Goofy used the Metro subway trains to travel around Paris. When they arrived at the Louvre Museum station, there were so many statues and paintings on display that Goofy thought they were already in the museum.

The Louvre Museum is one of the most famous museums in the world. It contains many great paintings and sculptures. Before it became a museum, it was used as a fort to guard against invaders of the city.

The French are known for their
wonderful pastries, such as
éclairs, napoleons, and fruit tarts.
Most people don't have as much
trouble as Goofy does eating
their éclairs, which are chocolate-topped
sweet pastries filled with lots of cream.

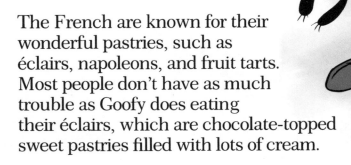

The Seine River divides Paris
neatly into two parts called the Left Bank and the Right Bank.
Many people like to take boat rides down the Seine.

Many of the same kinds
of lovely flowers that grow
in the Luxembourg Gardens in Paris
are grown in the southern part of France.
The flowers are used to make women's perfumes.

Au revoir means goodbye in French.